Dear Parent:
Your child's love of reading starts here!

I Can Read Books have introduced children to the joy of reading since 1957. Featuring award-winning authors and illustrators and a fabulous cast of beloved characters, I Can Read Books set the standard for beginning readers. From books your child reads with you to the first books they read alone, there are I Can Read Books for every stage of reading:

SHARED READING
Basic language, word repetition, and whimsical illustrations, ideal for sharing with your emergent reader

BEGINNING READING
Short sentences, familiar words, and simple concepts for children eager to read on their own

READING WITH HELP
Engaging stories, longer sentences, and language play for developing readers

READING ALONE
Complex plots, challenging vocabulary, and high-interest topics for the independent reader

ADVANCED READING
Short paragraphs, chapters, and exciting themes for the perfect bridge to chapter books

Every child learns in a different way and at their own speed. Some read through each level in order. Others go back and forth between levels and read favorite books again and again. You can help your young reader improve and become more confident by encouraging their own interests and abilities.

A lifetime of discovery begins with the magical words, "I Can Read!"

For Thompson Daniel and Anna Aurelia
—A.S.C.

ISBN 0-439-85328-1

Text copyright © 2005 by Alyssa Satin Capucilli. Illustrations copyright © 2005 by Pat Schories.
All rights reserved. Published by Scholastic Inc., 557 Broadway, New York, NY 10012,
by arrangement with HarperCollins Publishers. SCHOLASTIC and associated logos are
trademarks and/or registered trademarks of Scholastic Inc.

12 11 10 9 8 7 6 5 4 3 2 1   6 7 8 9 10 11/0

Printed in the U.S.A.   23

First Scholastic printing, January 2006

I Can Read Book® is a trademark of HarperCollins Publishers Inc.

MY FIRST

I Can Read Book®

Biscuit and the Baby

story by ALYSSA SATIN CAPUCILLI
pictures by PAT SCHORIES

SCHOLASTIC INC.

New York Toronto London Auckland Sydney
Mexico City New Delhi Hong Kong Buenos Aires

Woof, woof!

What does Biscuit see?

Woof, woof!

Biscuit sees the baby.

Biscuit wants
to meet the baby!

Woof, woof!

Sshhh! Quiet, Biscuit.

The baby is sleeping.

It's not time
to meet the baby yet.

Woof, woof!

Biscuit sees the baby's rattle.

Woof, woof!

Biscuit sees the baby's bunny.

Woof, woof!
Biscuit wants
to meet the baby!

Sshhh! Quiet, Biscuit.

The baby is still sleeping.

It's not time

to meet the baby yet.

Woof, woof!

Silly puppy!

That's not your blanket.

Oh no, Biscuit.
Those booties
are for the baby.
Woof, woof!

Funny puppy!

You want to meet the baby.

But it's not time

to meet the baby yet.

Woof!

Waa! Waa! Waa! Waa!

Woof! Woof! Woof! Woof!

Biscuit, come back.

It's only the baby!

Woof, woof!

Here, sweet puppy.
Now it's time
to meet the baby.
Woof, woof!

Best of all, it's time
for the baby to meet
a new friend!

Woof!

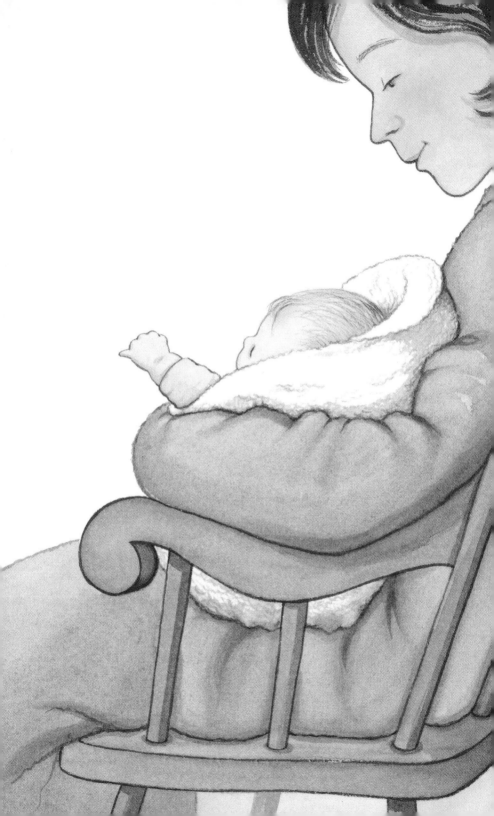